Running in the Corridors

Running in the Corridors

Seven Stories by Ann Thwaite

RETHINK PRESS

First Published in Great Britain 2014
by Rethink Press

Image for *Running in the Corridors,* 'Olga Writes a Letter' by Gwen Raverat © Raverat Ltd. Please see www.raverat.com to buy a print of this and other pictures by Gwen Raverat.

Images for *The Man on the Bicycle, Feeding the Cats, Happily Ever After, The Dog in the Watermeadow, The Picnic* and *Jack's Poem* by Cordelia Jones

Image for *At the Airport Hotel* by Christopher Orlando Page

Contents

Author's Note

THESE SEVEN STORIES WERE ALL WRITTEN LONG AGO, in a world without computers, the internet or even mobile phones.

Several of them were published in Macmillan anthologies in the seventies, edited by Marni Hodgkin, whose encouragement always meant so much to me as a writer, not least when I was working on my biographies. Some of them were broadcast as BBC Morning Stories.

For thirty or forty years the typescripts were all hidden in a file in my Norfolk study until Lucy McCarraher of Rethink Press showed an interest in them. I am grateful to her.

I am also grateful to my friend Penelope Lively, whose introduction will give the reader an idea of what to expect.

What might be unexpected is the ingenious poem I couldn't resist adding for the reader's pleasure. It was written when our eldest grandson was named in 1985. The book is dedicated to him and our other grandchildren, all of whom are now far older than the children in these stories:

Jack, **Will** and **Maisie**, **Toby**, **Dominic** and **Amy**,
Alex and **Emily, Joe** and **Eva**.

Introduction

HERE IS A COLLECTION OF STORIES which explore in different ways the perception and experience of the young. The various protagonists learn both about themselves and about the betraying nature of adult behaviour.

Running in the Corridors describes a boarding school girl's joyous experience of escaping constriction and discipline.

In *Feeding the Cats,* the teenage protagonist and her sister indulge their curiosity about some neighbours' intriguingly different lifestyle, and she ends up discovering her own capacity to do the right thing.

There is a nice instance of both cultural rapport and cultural difference in *At the Airport Hotel,* as a technicate American child comes to the aid of an elderly stranger.

But four stories explore the darker side of growing up, the bewildered observation of adult behaviour that is sometimes baffling, sometimes downright disturbing. A schoolgirl, warned by the head teacher about an 'unpleasant character' who is around, sees a man on a bicycle expose himself as he rides past her.

Thirteen-year-old Laura, in *Happily Ever After*, takes a sceptical view of marriage and refuses to be a bridesmaid at her aunt's wedding. But the wedding itself reveals something about her parents' marriage that is more crucially unsettling.

The Dog in the Water Meadow displays the dysfunctional family next door through the eyes of a fourteen-year old boy, witness to a wayward act of violence and the anguished wail of an adult driven to despair.

And adult chicanery is the subject of *The Picnic* – a woman lying rather than tell the truth to her wealthy neighbour lover, thus implicating horrified children.

Ann Thwaite is best known as the biographer of Frances Hodgson Burnett, Edmund and Philip Henry Gosse, Emily Tennyson and A. A. Milne, and it is good to have these early stories of hers, which have never been collected together, back in circulation. The period flavour is a pleasure, as is the way in which she can present a world seen through the eyes of her young characters with clarity and understanding.

Penelope Lively

Running in the Corridors

EVERY MORNING IT WAS THE SAME: the bed had to be stripped, right down to the mattress, and the whole lot – sheets, blankets, cover – hung over the plain deal chair that stood in every cubicle alongside the bed. There was no other place the chair could stand. Each cubicle was too small for individual variations in the furniture. Bed, chair, dressing table, wardrobe with a blue curtain instead of doors. That was all. Not even a desk. You did your prep with everyone else downstairs in the Prep Room. Rows of you; heads bent over books, shuffling your feet, itching, spilling ink as you dipped scratchy pens in the two ink-wells allowed to each table.

There was no chance of cheating over the bed-making. The stripping took place before breakfast; the making afterwards. During breakfast, while you ate pale grey porridge, flabby bacon and hard fried bread, Matron and her henchmen were on the prowl, dispensing order-marks. HAIRS IN BRUSH. DIRTY SOCKS UNDER BED. Disorder marks they should have been called.

Helen got plenty and few stars. Last week she had had the disgrace of carrying the house flag up to the platform in front of the whole school and depositing it in the drainpipe. That was what happened. Each week the stars and the order-marks were counted up and balanced. The flags of the top three houses stood with their poles in holes in a sort of flag-rack, the best one at the top. The three worst houses stood for the week in the drainpipe. It wasn't a symbolic drainpipe, but a bit of the real thing. Privately, Helen much preferred the shining stoneware drainpipe, gleaming like the best toffee, to the flimsy wooden rack for the winning flags.

Putting the bedclothes back on the thoroughly, unnecessarily, aired bed was an art. If you were tall and strong, it was possible to replace the whole lot at once, smooth them out, tuck them in and have done. Helen, the thinnest, shortest girl in her form (just four foot six inches in her lisle-stockinged feet), had to do it the hard way. Underblanket, bottom sheet, top sheet, two more blankets, blue cotton cover. Every morning. No normal person would think it necessary to strip a bed every morning. If she ever grew up, Helen felt sure she would never strip a bed again unless to put on clean sheets.

Certainly she might pull the top bedclothes back to allow the night's warmth to disappear. But more than that she would not do.

It seemed to Helen that this might be the effect of a lot of school rules. NO RUNNING IN THE CORRIDORS. NO TALKING AFTER LIGHTS OUT. Sometimes Helen saw a future of endless running – down pavements, through department stores, even in the corridors of town halls and in the aisles of cathedrals, in places where otherwise she might well have preferred to walk. Sometimes she saw a future of lying in bed beside a husband and being compelled to talk and talk, when otherwise she might well have loved or slept. Mostly, she saw no future at all, but felt herself trapped, static, caged by rules.

As, at last, she pulled the blue cover over the pillow and placed her old teddy bear in his regulation position, bang in the middle of the slope, the strange effect of this boarding-school life struck her again. In a real room, rich with a confusion of possessions, there would be no need for Ted. Here he had to occupy a central position. GIRLS ARE ALLOWED A SOFT TOY OR SIMILAR FRIENDLY FELLOW. No, they would not possibly say that. It must be an unwritten rule. There were plenty of those as well. And for good measure, Helen made up her own. IF YOUR PARENTS ARE DIVORCED, IT IS TACTFUL TO HAVE THEIR PHOTOS IN SEPARATE FRAMES, SO ONE OR OTHER MAY BE DISPLAYED AS APPROPRIATE.

At one end of Helen's dressing-table, at an exact angle of forty-five degrees to the glass, there was a photo of her mother, smiling slightly, with a double row of pearls and her hair smart from the hairdresser.

Her father's photo had been hidden in the top drawer on a number of occasions; her mother's never. Helen's father had never visited the school. She had not seen him since the divorce five years before. Her mother had once told her that he was in America. His name had not been mentioned for a long time.

Helen could hear Philippa and Rae talking over the partition that separated their cubicles.

'She had five slices of fried bread. I counted.'

'Greedy Pig…'

'She probably knew it's liver for lunch.'

'Ugh. All those veins.'

Food exercised their minds a great deal. Helen herself hardly ate, and had been prescribed Malt Extract as a supplement. She glanced at her watch. Eight-thirty. It was time she went along for it now.

There was a queue outside Matron's room of assorted girls waiting for their daily doses. Cough syrup, pills, strange pink medicines with nasty smells pretending to be raspberry. Malt Extract was all right and Helen licked the spoon for the last scrap. Matron looked at her approvingly.

'That's right. You'll soon put on a pound or two.'

At the weigh-in at the end of each term, Matron was personally affronted if you hadn't gained a suitable amount. She made that funny 'tch, tch' noise with her tongue and pushed back behind her ears endless threads of grey hair. 'You're not as bonny as we'd like,' she would always say to Helen. Matron's father had come from Scotland. 'Ye could do with a wee bit more flesh on you.' She patted her own starched front complacently. Helen was the only one left in her form who still showed no signs of turning into a woman. Lying in her twice-weekly bath (Tuesdays and Saturdays at 7.45 sharp), Helen would gaze at her flat chest with interest, almost expecting it to swell before her eyes. But it never did.

Ridding the roof of her mouth of the last morsel of sweetness, Helen doubted Matron's comforting words. It seemed unlikely she would ever put on a pound or two. Perhaps, she thought, I am a freak. A female Peter Pan. Thirteen years old and hair only on my head.

She went to clean her teeth in the wash-room, carefully choosing the fourth basin on the right as she always did. If you couldn't have a basin of your own, at least you could always use the same one. There was a fine crack running down from the base of the right-hand tap to the plug-hole. It was a hair-crack, only splitting the surface of the porcelain. When she washed her hair, swilling most of the loose hairs down the plug-hole, Helen always saved one long wet hair and pressed it from the base of the left-hand tap to the plug-hole, an exact twin of the real crack. It was never there when she returned.

She was spitting toothpaste foam into the basin when a prefect came in.

'Oh, there you are, Helen Watson; I've been looking for you everywhere.'

Helen wiped her mouth on the back of her hand. 'I was having my malt. I was cleaning my teeth,' she said defensively.

'All right, all right,' the prefect said. 'But you'd better cut along to Miss Herbert's study. She asked me to find you fifteen minutes ago.'

Helen shivered. What had she done now? Miss Herbert never saw girls before morning school unless it was something important. Could she have found out about Helen's hours of reading by torchlight under the hall platform when she should have been gardening? (Gardening meant weeding the flower-beds.) Could she have discovered the paper bags of disgusting school meat Helen had thrown away in the Prep Room waste-paper basket? Had she realised that Helen could not possibly have got through all the shoe-polish she had claimed in her account book? She looked down at her shoes. They weren't really clean now. Some of the earth from under the hall platform still clung to her heels. She took the handkerchief out of her pocket and rubbed at them. Her handkerchief was brown but the shoes looked much the same. She started to run and slowed again. NO RUNNING IN THE CORRIDORS.

'Come in Helen.' Miss Herbert was smiling. Her thin birdlike face was really smiling. It wasn't the cool, polite smile Helen was accustomed to. 'I have some rather exciting news for you, Helen. 'From your father. Do sit down, dear.'

Helen was glad to sit down. Her knees felt weak and strange.

'He is coming to see you. I've had a telegram. He will be in Wellington tomorrow, Friday. He wants you to spend the weekend with him at the Trafalgar.'

'The Trafalgar? I've never stayed in a hotel before.'

The Trafalgar was the biggest, smartest hotel in Wellington. Tables with starched white cloths and gleaming silver stood ankle-deep in thick carpet. Waiters appeared silently with enormous starched white menus and hovered discreetly at a distance so that you didn't feel they were in a hurry for your order.

'What's it to be, Helen?' her father asked her. 'Melon, grapefruit, tomato juice, minestrone... You name it, they've got it.'

Helen looked at her menu. Most of it was French, a French that seemed to have little in common with the French she learnt at school. Nothing resembled school.

It was a different world and had its own unreality. When she looked up again, she saw her father's eyes were still on the menu, staying there rather longer than was necessary, it seemed. The menu was long, but surely it was not essential to read every word. He must have often seen such menus before. He had walked about the hotel as one well used to hotel life.

She saw a man like a distant cousin of the man in the photograph on her school dressing-table: older, gentler, less defined. His hair, far from being close-cropped, was longer than that of most people's fathers, and his tie was now a rough olive tweed that looked well with the smooth light grey suit. There were two deep vertical lines between his eyebrows that had not been there before. He shut his eyes for a moment, no longer pretending to read the menu. Opening them, he looked up and caught her eye.

'It's fun to have a grown-up daughter to take out to dinner,' he said, smiling at her above his menu. They seemed to be using them as shields. When she had last seen him she was eight years old.

'I'm not grown-up,' Helen said, yet suddenly felt she was. She wanted to run her hand along her father's brow and smooth out the wrinkles as she had smoothed the cover of her bed. 'Why didn't you come before?'

'I've been in America,' he said. 'I couldn't come.'

'You could have written,' Helen murmured behind her menu.

'Your mother said…' He stopped, embarrassed. 'Well, what will you have?'

Helen smiled suddenly, understanding him, remembering him. 'I'll have an avocado pear.' She had never tasted one before but surely that was the right thing to have.

They relaxed then, eating and talking. Helen did not like the avocado, but she finished it completely. Its flesh was smooth and green and tasted slightly rotten. Afterwards, they had duck and orange with beans and French fried potatoes (Helen called them chips). And, last of all, a chocolate mousse. Helen had never eaten so much in her life.

They had bedrooms on the same corridor. Helen was pleased with hers. It was four times the size of her cubicle at school. There was a pretty orange wallpaper and a white telephone by her bed. In one corner a door led to her own bathroom. Helen filled the bath until the water touched the bottom of the overflow hole.

'Nine pm on a Friday,' she thought, watching the water overflow gently as she made waves with her hands. 'What a marvellous time to be having a bath.'

Next morning, when she got up, she pulled the bed-clothes back just enough to cool the warm place where her thin body had lain all night. When her father knocked and came in to see if she was ready for breakfast, Helen was making the bed.

'They have maids here to make the beds,' her father said.

'Oh, do they?' Helen was surprised. 'But I wanted to make it myself. My own way.' She smoothed out the bedspread.

'Sure,' he said. 'There's no harm in that. Ready for breakfast?' Helen nodded. 'I'll call up the lift.' And she ran along the hotel corridor, smiling.

The Man on the Bicycle

IT WAS EARLY NOVEMBER, that grey time when the summer is forgotten and Christmas still far away. A cold wind blew an empty crisps packet briskly across the playground and stirred the damp piles of leaves. But the school hall was too hot, crammed as it was with six hundred girls, shuffling, whispering, yawning, itching. Miss Hammond came in. The headmistress, in a neat blue skirt and jersey, walked up the aisle between the six hundred green girls. They all wore the green school uniform and smiled when they sang, as they did from time to time, 'O all ye Green Things upon the earth, bless ye the Lord, praise Him and magnify Him forever.'

The whispering and shuffling subsided but the itching and yawning went on. Clare Fuller's fingers, running along the smooth metal frame of the chair she sat in, touched something alien – an excrescence, that was the word – a lump of someone's disgusting chewing gum stuck to the metal. Clare shuddered. It was strange. Chewing gum, like spit, was all right inside your own mouth but outside it was nasty. A favourite phrase of her mother's ran through her head. 'A place for everything and everything in its place.' Miss Hammond's voice unexpectedly interrupted her thoughts. Normally they started the morning assembly with a hymn but this morning Miss Hammond was talking.

'...before we start singing, there is something rather serious I want to talk to you about.' The girls shifted in their chairs and glanced at each other with exaggeratedly raised eyebrows. 'After you all went home last night I had a visit from a police officer and he gave me some rather disturbing information. It seems there is an unpleasant character hanging about the area.' Miss Hammond was not specific about what made him unpleasant. 'The police have particularly requested that if any of you have to stay late for music lessons, rehearsals, club meetings and so on, you should not walk home alone in the dark. I am cancelling all after-school activities for today and until further notice. The younger ones at any rate should ask their mothers to meet them or make other arrangements.' There was a murmur round the hall. 'Quiet now. There is nothing to be alarmed about, but it is as well to be careful. If anything unusual occurs you are to ring the police as soon as you can and report the matter… Now we will go on as usual. The hymn is number 246: "Angel voices ever singing".' The unangelic voices rose and fell.

For Clare Fuller and her form that morning the first lesson was Geography. Miss Dyer, the elderly Geography teacher, looked pinker than usual. 'She's thinking about the man,' Clare whispered to her friend, Sally.

'What was that Clare?' Miss Dyer asked. 'If you have something interesting to say we might as well all hear it.'

'I was talking about the Man… ' Clare began honestly. The form giggled. Clare's courage failed her. 'I was talking about the Manitoba area,' she continued and then realised they were supposed to be studying the eastern coast of the United States and wherever the Manitoba area was, it certainly wasn't there. 'I mean I'm sorry, Miss Dyer, I was talking about the Manhattan Island.'

'Oh, indeed, Clare. And what can you tell us about the Manhattan Island?' She put the stress gently on the definite article.

'It's the island New York stands on. I suppose it's the most densely populated island in the world but maybe Hong Kong is. It's… it's…' She sought desperately for inspiration. 'It's a concrete jungle. It's very dangerous to walk there alone after dark.'

'All right, Clare. Thank you. I think we will concentrate now on the more purely geographic aspects of the eastern seaboard of the United States of America.' The lesson droned on.

They could not talk properly until break. Then speculation was intense.

'I wonder how the police know. I mean if he's already done something surely they'll arrest him.'

'Perhaps they just thought they saw the flash of a knife under his coat.'

'You can be arrested for that, carrying an offensive weapon. You don't have to *use* it.'

'Perhaps he doesn't have a weapon. Perhaps he just likes to jump out on people and frighten them.'

'It may be their purses he's after. I'm going to leave my Christmas money at home.'

'He's probably a sexual maniac with a passion for schoolgirls. I bet he's entranced by our green uniforms. They turn him on, I haven't a doubt.'

Clare listened to the conversations eddying around the form-room. In that familiar room, the subject was exciting not alarming. The man seemed, not a figure of menace, but someone sent to dispel the November boredom, to provide a fresh topic of conversation, to unite the girls and make them forget their usual bickerings and animosities.

Clare always walked home alone. She lived quite near the school, eight minutes' walk away, less in the morning if she were late and hurrying. Sally had to catch a bus and none of Clare's other friends lived in her direction. That afternoon she walked briskly – glad of the back of a sixth-former only a short distance ahead and of women with shopping baskets and prams. There was nearly always someone about. There was no need to feel alarmed.

If only she knew exactly what it was about the man which made him an 'unpleasant character'. Unpleasant was a rather weak word for Miss Hammond to use. Clare knew plenty of unpleasant people – Mr Phillips next door, for a start, always grumbling if he heard her pop records through the wall. She had to turn her record player so low she could hardly hear them herself. He was an unpleasant character, but the police would not be likely to send out a warning about him. Then there was Liz Raymond at school – always pouring cold water on any suggestion anyone else made, looking down her Roman nose, acting so cool you could scream. There was nothing pleasant about her. And Mrs Jennings at the corner shop, always so polite and smiling to the adults, but hurrying up the little kids from the junior school, pushing them into buying lots of junk they didn't really want (plastic toys that broke two minutes later) just so she could take their pennies and hustle them out of the shop. There were plenty of unpleasant people about.

It began to rain. Clare pulled up the hood of her duffle coat and looked around. The chestnut at the end of the lane was black against the sky. A few leaves still clung to the lower branches, thin and yellow like bunches of inedible bananas. The sixth-former had turned down a side-street. The shopping women had disappeared. The lane was now quite empty – long and grey and cold. It would be dark soon. Clare started to run, telling herself she wanted to get home before she was really wet. But her heart was behaving oddly and her knees felt weak and she knew that the rain was not the only reason she wished she were already home.

It was then she saw the man on his bicycle. He was riding towards her on the same side of the lane. He was wearing an old grey raincoat, so long that she wondered it did not catch in the spokes of the bicycle wheel. She found herself slowing down to a walk. Everything happened so slowly. It was like the slow-motion action replay you sometimes see on television. But the picture was different. It stayed etched on her mind's eye forever.

As the man came towards her, he pulled back his coat and she saw that the zip of his fly was undone and there, hanging down, were his private parts, like a frightened white creature exposed to the rain and cold. A poor little thing.

Clare stopped, appalled. She did not see the man's face, the strange look on his face. She thought she might scream but no sound came and in a moment the man on the bicycle had passed her. There was nothing to scream about. The lane was as quiet and grey as it had ever been. No screams, no violence, no knives, no blood. Only the 'unpleasant character' on his bicycle, the small man cycling off down the lane, with only one hand on his handle-bars now and his raincoat once more clutched to him. Clare looked at his back as he rode away and felt quite calm. But the tears were running down her cheeks.

She turned the corner, pushed through her own gate, opened her back door. Her mother was in the kitchen icing a cake. She looked up and saw Clare's face.

'Oh, darling… What's happened? Are you all right?' The knife, chocolate icing on its blade, fell to the ground. Clare's mother put her arms around her.

Clare pushed her gently away. She watched the knife spinning round, then stooped to pick it up. She washed it carefully under the hot tap. 'I'm perfectly all right. There's nothing wrong with me. I'm crying for someone else.' She went through the kitchen, hung up her coat in the hall, passed the phone at the bottom of the stairs without a glance and went up to her room, drying her damp cheeks on the sleeve of her green jersey.

'I'll bring you a cup of tea,' her mother called. 'I'm just making one. And there's your favourite cake.'

'Thanks,' Clare called back, 'I'll make a start on my homework. We've got a stack of it tonight.' She turned on her light and drew the curtains on the dark world outside.

Feeding the Cats

I WANT TO TELL YOU ABOUT THE WORST THING I have ever done. I have to tell someone or it will go round and round in my head forever, and drive me mad, I shouldn't be surprised. I've put the words 'Feeding the cats' at the beginning because that was the beginning. Feeding the cats or not feeding them was not the worst thing. I haven't got a cat's death on my conscience. They were just as sleek and healthy at the end of the week as they were when it started, those two. Macavity and Gus they were called. They used to come and rub against our legs and purr in a strange, loud way, as if we had turned on a switch; it really didn't sound natural.

I wasn't used to cats and I really liked it, them rubbing themselves against my legs and purring. But I suppose they only did it because they were hungry and knew we'd give them food. Cupboard love, in fact. The cats belonged to the Ravens, a rich young couple who lived in the big house across the road from us. They were as sleek and plump as their own cats, and as dark and glossy as their name. There they were, the two black, sleek cats living with the two black-haired, well-fed young people on one side of the road.

I lived on the other side of the road with my sister, Jackie, and our parents, who were not sleek and glossy at all, but always tired and sometimes irritable. They were wardens of an Old People's Home and we weren't allowed any pets because Mum said she had quite enough to do with Jackie and me and fourteen old ladies and gents, without having animals as well. I thought the old ladies and gents would like a cat about the place, but Mum wasn't having it and you couldn't really blame her. 'The place is like a zoo already,' she said one day. And I could see what she meant, with the old people sitting and staring, almost as if they were in cages, and the strange smell that you couldn't quite get rid of, however much lavender wax you rubbed into the furniture.

When Mrs Raven came over one evening, Jackie and I were really curious. We were upstairs at the time, doing our homework, and we peered over the banisters and saw her in the hall below. We'd never seen her to talk to, just on the other side of the road, a glimpse of her at her window, or in the car (sleek and glossy, of course). But Mum had apparently exchanged a few words with her from time to time, passed the time of day, as they say, and now Mrs Raven was coming to ask us a favour. She and her husband were going to America for a week and would it be possible, she just wondered, for Mum's two girls to cross the road twice a day and feed her two cats, Macavity and Gus. She could take them to a cattery, of course, but they would rather stay at home with their own familiar things around them. There was a little cat flap in the back door and they could come and go as it pleased them. Mrs Raven would be very grateful and would bring us a nice present from America. Well, of course, Jackie and I walked downstairs at that point and said we'd be ever so glad to help Mrs Raven. The fact was that we'd always wanted to see inside that house. From the outside, it looked like an advertisement on the telly for glossy paint or lawn mowers or something and the inside would be bound to be worth seeing. It was a golden opportunity.

To tell you the truth, my life at that time was a bit boring. There seemed to be nothing to it but home and school, school and home. And as home was full of old people and school full of old teachers, it was really nice to have something to make a change in our routine. We went home with Mrs Raven there and then, and she showed us what to give to the cats. They came in the moment we got there and twined themselves around our legs with that odd purr. Mrs Raven introduced us. 'Macavity and Gus, meet Lyn and Jackie. It's short for Asparagus.'

That kitchen was fantastic. Acres of formica. Eye-level grills, split-level ovens, infra-red spits, liquidisers, coffee-grinders… Mum didn't have half their gadgets though she was cooking for eighteen and there were only two of them and the cats. But we weren't to cook for the cats. All we had to do was to open cans on the super-automatic wall-hung magnetic can-opener (she showed us how to use it) and give them a can of Choosy or Felix or Tastee in the evenings (being careful to alternate meaty-flavoured and fishy-flavoured so they didn't get bored) and a bowlful of Whiskas, Munch or Kattee Krunch (liver, chicken or herring-flavoured) in the mornings.

The enormous refrigerator would be left on to hold the pint of milk the milkman would deliver every second day. They were not great milk drinkers, Macavity and Gus, but they liked a little every now and again and it would have to go in the fridge because they wouldn't touch it if it were turned, and the room would be quite warm. Mrs Raven would leave the central heating on ('It'll only use a teeny bit of oil,' she said, laughing apologetically), so that the pipes wouldn't freeze and the cats would have a warm place to retire to when they had wearied of outdoor exploration. The only other thing we had to do was to wash out the bowls. ('They practically wash themselves with their rough little tongues,' Mrs Raven said, laughing again.)

She gave us a key, with a smart blue and silver label on it saying BACK DOOR, and told us to come for the first time three days later on the Monday evening. 'We shall be over Greenland's icy mountains, by then,' she said.

Lucky old you, I thought, but all I said was, 'I hope you have a nice time, Mrs Raven.' Very politely. 'Don't worry about your cats.' I bent down to stroke Gus (or it might have been Macavity; I couldn't really tell the difference) so she could see I was going to do my duties affectionately as well as efficiently.

'You will be sure to lock up carefully.' Mrs Raven said, suddenly worried. 'I really can trust you, can I?'

'Oh yes,' Jackie and I said together. She's only eleven and she'd been hopping around from foot to foot all the time Mrs Raven and I were talking. I could see she was dying to explore the house, but Mrs Raven didn't notice. 'Goodnight,' we said.

We could hardly wait until six on Monday evening. When at last it was time to feed the cats, I took the key out of my purse and said, 'Do come in, Jacqueline. It's delightful to see you here. You must meet my cats, Macavity and Gus.'

The two cats had gone in through their special flap and were standing expectantly by their bowls. I opened the cupboard doors with a flourish and they came over and rubbed against my legs. 'Now, what would you like?' I read the labels on a different shelf from the cat food. 'Stuffed vine leaves, chestnut purée, artichoke hearts, whole sweet red peppers, ravioli, Alaskan King Crab, Gazpacho soup…' There seemed no end to the exotic and delicious things in that cupboard. Well, I supposed they were delicious. I hadn't tasted half of them.

'Fishy-flavoured Felix, please,' Jackie said. So I took down the can and opened it on the super-automatic wall-hung magnetic can opener and tipped the mush into the cats' blue bowls – they matched the formica exactly. While I was spooning out the last fragments, I noticed Jackie had slipped out of the door and into the next room.

'It's fabulous!' she shouted. I followed her, leaving the cats to get on with their supper. She had taken off her shoes and was walking joyfully all over the floor of the living room, almost up to her ankles, it seemed, in the long pile of the camel-coloured carpet. 'It's the most beautiful carpet in the world! It's an Ideal Home. Look, Lyn. Isn't it gorgeous?'

And the room was gorgeous. There were brilliant orange chrysanthemums on the curtains and piles of plump orange cushions on the two settees. Everything else was quietly coloured: cream, straw, buff, beige. Along one wall, there was a hi-fi stereo system and a great colour telly with doors to hide the screen. I sat down and said grandly 'Do sit down, Jacqueline. You must be tired.' Jackie sank down onto the other settee and gave a great yawn 'Some people are lucky,' she said. She looked longingly at the door that led to the rest of the house, but I said, 'Mum will be wondering where we've got to.' I patted the cushions to remove the signs of our bodies and ran my hand over the long pile of the carpet.

Each day was the same. The mornings weren't much fun as we were always in a rush and nearly late for school. Either Jackie or I, whoever was ready first, just dashed across the road, washed up the bowls and tipped some Munch or Krunch into one blue bowl and some milk into the other. But in the evenings, it was different. We lingered. We explored. We played games, always making sure that we left everything as we found it. Mum was so busy getting the old people their high tea (we had supper by ourselves at seven) that she never seemed to notice whether we'd been five minutes or fifty.

It was on the fourth evening that we first went into Mr and Mrs Raven's bedroom.

'Fabulous.' Jackie said. It was her favourite word. The bed was the biggest bed I had ever seen.

'It must be six feet across.' I said.

'Seven,' Jackie said.

The room was surrounded with mirrors, so that it seemed to go on forever. There were cupboards all along one wall with mirrors on every door. We opened them to increase the odd reflections, the numerous images of ourselves that surrounded us. One of the cupboards was full of narrow drawers, each one neatly labelled. 'Bras, Pants, Stockings, Trash…' I was reading them out to Jackie and hesitated at the curious word trash.

'What's trash?' Jackie asked.

'Who steals my purse steals trash,' I quoted. We had just been doing *Othello* at school and the phrase had stuck in my mind. 'Rubbish, it means rubbish.' I remembered our old English teacher saying it as if she'd said it a million times before.

'Rubbish?' Jackie said. 'She wouldn't keep rubbish in a bedroom drawer. Have a look, Lyn.'

I hesitated. I really did hesitate. Every day as we'd gone from room to room, tested the Ravens' chairs as if we were Goldilocks, admired their taste in textiles, read out the titles of their books, we had not yet opened any drawers, or cupboards, except the kitchen cupboards and that was part of the job.

But I opened the drawer marked Trash. Mrs Raven would never know. She was hundreds of miles away, drinking highballs on Broadway, or whatever it was people did when they went to America. The drawer was full of cheap bangles and necklaces; there were dozens of strings of wooden beads and shells and coloured seeds. It wasn't jewellery; you couldn't call it jewellery.

Jackie was sitting on the dressing table stool and I took one of the strings of beads – they were wooden ones, painted a bright turquoise – and put it round her neck. It looked good on the navy blue of her school jersey. I put a string of orange shells round my own neck and we stood there, twisting and turning and watching our reflections in the mirrors. Suddenly I noticed the time; it was already ten to seven and Mum would be bound to ask awkward questions if we were not back in time for supper.

We pushed in the drawer, shut the mirror doors neatly and removed all traces of our visit to the bedroom. 'Bathroom tomorrow,' Jackie said, as we locked the back door and gave Macavity and Gus a farewell stroke. 'I've been saving up the bathroom. I bet it's fabulous.'

We were in the shabby old bathroom at home, giving our hands a quick wash before supper, when I noticed the beads we were still wearing. 'She won't miss them,'

I said. She had so many of them; she had so much. I took the two strings of beads and shoved them in the top drawer of the chest in our bedroom. Then we went down to supper.

I didn't feel in the least guilty. We continued to behave in the Ravens' house in exactly the same way – enjoying the softness of the carpets, the warmth, the beauty, the feeling of being in another world. The house was our reward for feeding the cats. We seemed to rub against the comfort of the house, just as the cats rubbed against our legs, purring.

On the fifth evening, we went into the bathroom and it *was* fabulous. I saw Jackie looking longingly at the enormous bath and at a great jar of green bubble stuff, pine-scented, on a glass shelf above the basin.

'No you don't,' I said. 'That's going too far.'

The sixth evening was our last. We decided to have a dinner party. I went upstairs and walked down again to greet Jackie as she came across the hall.

'How lovely to see you, Jacqueline.'

We sat at the rosewood table in the dining room, sipping from imaginary wine-glasses and making polite conversation.

'Very cold for the time of year,' Jackie said.

'Most unseasonable,' I agreed. 'But the days are lengthening. Have you heard the first cuckoo?'

'Cuckoo! Cuckoo!'

I joined in. We were whirling and dancing. We were full of the joys of Spring. The cats, who had finished their supper, came in to see what we were up to. Jackie picked up Macavity and I picked up Gus. And we danced round and round with them in our arms.

'We need music,' Jackie said. 'Let's see what they've got.'

We looked at the Ravens' records. They had hundreds; everything from *Yellow Brick Road* to Beethoven's Ninth.

'Some people are lucky,' Jackie said, not for the first time, lifting the lid of the hi-fi, but I said 'No,' sharply. 'It's time we were going.' And it really was. The Ravens would be back early next morning. I walked quickly through the house for the last time, making sure everything was in order. We said good-bye to the cats and went home to our own supper.

Mrs Raven came in the next evening, full of smiles, and gave Jackie and me a key-ring each, with our names, Jackie and Lyn, on little labels like American car number plates, and a big box of candy. She said the cats were in splendid form and she was so grateful. We smiled and said it had been a pleasure. It really had.

We didn't suppose we would see Mrs Raven again, except in her car or on the other side of the road, but two weeks later, on a Saturday, I came in with the orange shells round my neck (well, there was no point in leaving them lying in a drawer, was there?) and there she was, in our kitchen, talking to Mum.

'Hullo Lyn,' she said, all smiles. 'I was just asking your mother…' She stopped smiling. She had noticed the shells. 'That's funny,' she said. 'I have some shells just like that… Do you find yourself fiddling with them?'

'Yes, I do,' I said, fiddling with them like mad. If they had been a rosary, I could have said a prayer.

'Where did you get them?' Mum asked. 'New, are they?'

'Yes,' I mumbled. 'Jane was tired of them and said I could have them.' Jane was a friend of mine. It seemed to me, at that moment, that if I was a thief, I might as well be a liar too.

I could see Mrs Raven was dying to get home and check if her own orange shells were still in the drawer marked Trash. In a few moments, she made an excuse and left.

I slipped upstairs, pulled the shells off my neck and the wooden beads out of the drawer. I shoved them in an old brown envelope, wrote 'Mrs Raven' on the outside, and beneath it the words, 'I'm sorry'. Then, without giving myself time to think, I rushed across the road and pushed the packet through the Ravens' letterbox.

Macavity came round the corner of the house and rubbed against my legs. He obviously couldn't tell a liar and a thief when he saw one. I bent down to stroke him. 'No Kattee Krunch, I'm afraid,' I whispered sadly in his ear. 'I shan't be asked to feed the cats again.'

Happily Ever After

EVERYONE SEEMED OBSESSED BY WEDDINGS and marriages that year. There was the Royal Wedding for a start, with pictures of Prince Charles and Lady Di on every tea towel and every mug. You couldn't turn on the radio without hearing who had been invited (Harry Secombe) and who hadn't (a paralysed policeman) and who had turned down the invitations anyway (Barbara Cartland and the King and Queen of Spain). And as if that wasn't enough, there was the reaction to Shula calling off her wedding on *The Archers*, just to remind you that marriage was still supposed to be the be-all and end-all of every girl's existence, however much the Women's Movement might deplore the fact.

Polly Toynbee in the *Guardian* interviewed a class of sixteen-year-old girls in Birmingham and found that they all expected to be married by the time they were twenty-four. 'It's the way we've been brought up,' one of them said.

Not that Laura Powell's parents had brought her up differently. If you had talked to them, they would certainly have said they hoped that Laura (now thirteen) would find the man who would make her happy before ten years were up. Her mother, who was very fond of small children, might even have admitted that she was looking forward to her grandchildren. Laura was the youngest; her two older brothers (though not yet married) had long since left home to make their way in the world. One had done a degree in business studies and was now working for a manufacturer of double-glazing units; the other was living on the dole in Southampton, having trained to be a teacher and given up after filling in his fourth job application form.

Each time either brother (they were called Derek and Graham) brought home a girlfriend, their mother would size them up and wonder. Of course, Graham (he was the trained teacher) couldn't marry until he had a job, but it really was high time Derek (he was the one in double-glazing) settled down. Laura was tired of hearing her mother speculate on each new girlfriend's chances.

Mrs Powell had given up speculating about Mr Powell's much younger sister, Sylvia. Sylvia was nearly forty and seemed well settled into the life of a successful career woman. She owned a secondhand bookshop in Hammersmith, a small but thriving concern with particularly good sections on the Women's Movement, topography and out-of-print fiction. Customers came from all over London and two or three times a year Sylvia Powell published a catalogue which had customers all over the world. Laura often went down to help on Saturdays and in the holidays, and between serving customers, read her way steadily along the shelves until she was undoubtedly one of the best read thirteen-year-olds in West London. Ask her about the novels of Rosamund Lehmann or Elizabeth Bowen or who had written on women's place in classical Greece and she could certainly tell you, with style and verve. You could say that Sylvia Powell's bookshop was an influence to counteract the normal influence of Laura's own mother.

'I shall be like you,' Laura said to Sylvia one day when the shop was empty and they were carefully sharing a Cornish pasty made by Laura's mother. 'I shall never marry.' If Laura had been looking at her aunt and not at the piece of Cornish pasty she was cutting, she might have seen Sylvia Powell blush.

'Don't you be so sure,' was all Sylvia said. And it was only a few weeks later that one of her regular customers, a schoolmaster widower in his fifties asked Sylvia to be his wife. She agreed – for reasons it is not necessary to go into here.

Laura was hurt and puzzled when Sylvia eventually told her the news.

'I didn't think you'd be like everyone else. Why does love have to be legalised?' Laura said. 'Marriage is so boring. Two people locked together forever; never allowed to look at any one else. What will happen to Jack and Philip?' she named two of her aunt's friends who often came to the shop just as it was closing and drank a friendly glass of beer.

'We'll still be friends,' Sylvia said. 'Hugo won't mind.' She named the man she had decided to marry.

'Oh yes he will,' Laura said gloomily. 'And you'll mind if he goes off and has lunch with other women.'

'Yes, I suppose I will,' Sylvia admitted.

'Why does it always have to be two by two?' Laura asked. 'Mum and Dad said everything they had to say to each other years ago.'

'Nonsense,' Sylvia said. 'Well, anyway, they'll have plenty to talk about when I tell them I'm going to marry Hugo.'

'Oh yes; they'll like that. Especially Mum. She *loves* weddings and there hasn't been one for ages… '

'And you'll be my bridesmaid,' Sylvia said, looking quizzically at Laura. 'In green, I think.'

'Oh, no, I won't,' Laura said. 'Not in any colour.'

They all tried to persuade her. Her mother tried every approach – bribing, weeping, pleading. It was ridiculous. Sylvia was much cooler about the whole thing, but even she wouldn't accept Laura's refusal and believed persuasion would finally make her change her mind. Her father pleaded too, if only because he liked a quiet life. Even Derek and Graham were roped in to suggest that Laura stopped being so eccentric. Most girls would love to have the chance to be a bridesmaid. Hugo would undoubtedly give her a present. She would have a lovely dress for wearing afterwards to parties.

'I don't like parties,' Laura said. It was true.

She would not change her mind. And when she discovered that Hugo, that middle-aged bridegroom, actually had five-year old twin granddaughters (sensible small girls who could be relied on), everyone finally accepted her stand.

'You know I've not got anything against you and Hugo,' Laura said awkwardly one morning as she tied up a parcel of books for her aunt. 'It's only marriage I'm against.'

In fact she had come to like Hugo a lot. He was an interesting man who had published a couple of novels. He had the knack of making Laura feel interesting too. But she still hated to think of the two of them, day after day, for the rest of their lives, eating breakfast together, declining into the routine relationships she saw all around her. When he wasn't working, her father did nothing but play golf and bridge. She doubted whether in years he'd asked her mother for anything more important than the marmalade or a clean shirt. As for her mother, she seemed happily taken up with her work for the Citizen's Advice Bureau and Meals on Wheels. She seemed hardly to notice her husband, though she would certainly have missed him if he'd not been there.

Laura agreed to go to the wedding. Like her father, perhaps she really preferred a quiet life. She had made her stand. She would not take part in the ceremony. But she realised how hurt everyone would be if she refused to go altogether.

There were relations coming up from Cornwall – dozens of them she hadn't seen for ages. Her aunt and her father had grown up together near Fowey. The photo album was full of Cornish scenes and the uncle and aunts and cousins who would come on the night train for Sylvia's late joy. Their mother had died when they were young – but their father was still alive, and happy to 'give away' the middle-aged daughter who had in fact gone away from him so long before.

'Remind me what they all look like,' Laura had begged her father – but there were no recent photos. The most recent albums were full of Laura and her brothers.

'Everyone has changed,' her father said turning over the pages of an early album. 'That was thirty years ago, Sylvia was nine years old.' Laura stared at the child with plaited hair and the cousins in baggy shorts and smocked dresses. 'That's Mary and Rachel and Jonathan – they're all coming.'

'And that's you,' Laura said, pointing at her father aged twenty or so, quite recognisable though with so much more hair.

'And who is that? Remind me,' Laura pointed at the girl with her father. She loved to see him blush.

'You know. That was Jenny Price, the girl I loved in my first year at university. She lived near London and I took her down to Cornwall several times to meet everyone. She loved it. She'd never been in Cornwall before. She was an only child and she loved us all. We swam and walked along the cliffs…' He paused. 'It's a long time ago.'

Laura knew the story perfectly well but she liked to hear it again and to imagine a time when her father loved someone else and she, Laura, might so easily never have existed. It made her feel the extraordinary luck of being precisely herself, against all the odds. She looked a long time at the photograph, thirty years old, black and white, remote.

***

The wedding day was brilliantly sunny. Laura awoke with no regrets for the green dress or the role-playing. She had agreed to hand out service papers at the back of the church, mainly because it would give her a good chance to look at all the guests. Hugo's list had some interesting names – a number of them Laura knew from the spines of books in the shop. And it would be fun to see all those Cornish relations. One or two of them had not been to London since her own christening more than twelve years before. Some she remembered from Cornish holidays – a picnic on the beach at Perranporth, a visit to a farm near Penzance. But the images from the thirty-year-old photograph album were stronger than the remembered faces. So that it was quite a shock when Jonathan's family arrived and she saw, not an eleven-year-old boy in shorts, but a middle-aged man in a dark suit, his hair as thin as her father's, and with him his wife and a couple of children, excited by their London visit.

The congregation gathered. They had given up the idea of having the bride's friends and relations on one side of the church, the bridegroom's on the other. That was always embarrassing if one seemed to have many more friends than the other. Laura handed out the service sheets; the ushers showed people where there was still room. It was getting towards noon. Hugo and his best man arrived. They looked distinguished and relaxed. Laura wondered momentarily about Hugo's earlier dead wife and hoped Sylvia would match his memories of her.

The organist began playing. There was a flurry of whispers, a happy murmur from the porch and Sylvia, her father and the two small bridesmaids started walking up the aisle. At that moment, Laura, who was waiting at the back to provide service sheets for any latecomers, noticed a woman, who must have come in by a side door, standing in the far aisle apparently reading the inscription on a memorial tablet.

As the bridal procession went up the centre of the church, the strange woman slipped inconspicuously into a seat at the back. Laura could only see her back – the grey and black striped dress she was wearing, her dark hair turning a little grey. She went over to give the woman a service paper and as the stranger turned towards her with a smile, Laura felt a shock of recognition. This was someone she had seen before. But where? She supposed, as she joined in the singing of the first hymn, it must be one of the Cornish relations, dimly remembered from a distant holiday. She glanced along the row; the woman was at the far end. The words of the marriage service itself were in her ears now. Hugo and Sylvia being joined together, locked, legally, officially, till death did them part. It seemed as if the bride were a sort of sacrifice before an altar to a God in which she did not really believe.

'Cleaving only to each other, so long as ye both shall live.'

And then Laura knew where she has seen that face before – not in Cornwall. Not indeed in the flesh. But in that black and white photograph, that thirty-year-old photograph which made her father blush and speak sweetly of his long lost love.

How extraordinary! But now that she had made the connection, there could be no possible doubt about it. What was she called? Jenny Price; that was it, or had been. Perhaps she had herself been married in the interval. Jenny Someone or Other, anyway. She had really changed very little – just older, a little lined, the hair a little grey, but still worn in the same style, fringed, short. What was she doing at Sylvia's wedding?

Laura worked it out as the singing of the second hymn rose and fell. 'Love divine all loves excelling.' (Did they really believe that? It seemed a bit defeatist on such an occasion.) Of course, Laura thought, her father's friend would have known them all thirty years before from those idyllic holidays. Sylvia herself, (the nine-year-old sister), Laura's grandfather, old Mr Powell, the cousins from the next farm, Mary, Rachel and Jonathan – and her father himself, the boy she had loved so long ago.

Laura thought she must have seen the newspaper announcement: At St Barnabas Church, Perivale, on September 10th, 1981, at noon, Sylvia Powell to Hugo Cummings. Friends welcome at the church.

The name Sylvia Powell must have caught her eye, and curiosity to see again after thirty years those familiar faces from her youth – and the new unfamiliar faces of her old love's wife and children – must have brought her to the church that day, slipping in inconspicuously, imagining after all that time that no one would recognise her.

But if Laura had, from the photograph, how much more would her father if he saw her there in the pew as he walked down the aisle with Hugo's married daughter on his arm. It would give him the most terrible shock, even a heart attack possibly. Such a ghost from his past.

Laura's heart was thumping so much she was surprised that Sylvia's friend Jack in the row in front didn't turn round to see what all the noise was about. The service was nearly over. The newly married pair, the best man, Laura's grandfather and her parents, Hugo's daughter and granddaughters had all gone out to the vestry. Then the organist crashed into the Mendelssohn Wedding March and the procession started down the aisle.

Laura watched her father as he got near the back of the church. She followed every movement of his eyes. Would he see what she had seen? The twenty-year-old face transformed into that of a woman of fifty. He did. But there was no trace of shock, not even of surprise. For a second his eyes met the woman's. He smiled slightly, a relaxed, conspiratorial extremely small smile which no one else would possibly have noticed. It was, Laura knew, the smile of someone seeing someone he expected to see, someone he had last seen not thirty years ago but perhaps last week.

'Until death do us part', 'cleaving only unto each other', 'forsaking all others' – the exclusive, locking, menacing words echoed in Laura's ears as she watched the woman leave the pew and slip out through the side door. Laura shut her eyes for a moment as if the sudden blankness could make her mind equally blank.

Then she went out of the church to join her family.

At the Airport Hotel

IF YOU HAD BEEN THERE, as I was, you would have noticed them too – the American family sitting at the last table on the hotel terrace in Basra, with limp straws and half-empty bottles of Pepsi in front of them. Were they American? I supposed so, straining to catch the sound of their voices. Everything is a question of observation in a hotel. The different groups sit separate and alone. There is no mingling, no communication. At first glance it may seem like a party – the drinking, the air of animation – but no one comes up and says, 'Didn't I see you at Peter's last week?' No one introduces you to anyone else.

But there *was* a party, a wedding party, coming out of the hotel, across the terrace and exploding into the garden, out among the tamarisk trees, the bougainvillea, hibiscus and jacaranda, all those exotic-sounding trees, into the air sweet with the smell of orange blossom. There was laughter and rhythm. Two children had drums. In the street, earlier in the day, I had seen a man making that sort of drum, stretching some sort of animal skin over the pottery shell. The children were beating the taut skin with practised fingers. Women were ululating, that strange exultant sound never heard in colder climates. A boy started dancing, swaying in time to the drumbeats. Hands clapped in the same rhythm.

A man threw sweets and children scrambled for them, eager to grab as many as they could. The grass was covered with the bright, scattered wrappings as they crammed the sweets into their mouths.

Two of the three American children (were they American?) watched the scene with envy. I could see what they wanted: not the sweets – their travelling bags, their hand luggage, contained plenty of sweets, along with their comics and felt pens and colouring books. What they wanted was to join in. For them, as for me, there was nothing to do but watch. They were on the outside, travelling through, passing by, uninvolved.

Their father said something. I couldn't catch what he said or even if it was English he used. But it was probably something meaning 'We should have some exercise', for they rose from their plastic and metal chairs, took up their hand luggage (denim bags, each neatly labelled) and walked past me, so close I could see the pink uncomfortable mosquito bites on the children's bare ankles. They went down the steps of the terrace and into the garden, under the trailing boughs of the brilliant bougainvillea.

The wedding party occupied the whole of the first lawn. The supplies of sweets were exhausted now, but the children still chewed. The wrappings lay on the grass like confetti, like petals. Two of the guests had cameras and the bride and groom smiled at them. The bride's white European dress looked a startling white against the black robes of the other women, against her own brown skin. The bridegroom's suit was new and uncomfortable.

The American family lingered on the path, admiring the scene. From my seat on the terrace above them, I looked at them. I said you would have noticed them too, if you'd been there. The reason was their colour. Can I mention colour? It is a dangerous subject. But the fact was it was their ludicrous paleness that marked them as they walked in the bright sunlight. They could not pretend to belong.

I am dark-haired myself, sallow and inconspicuous. I could be almost anything: Jew, Arab, Celt. No one looks at me twice. But this blonde family looked unnatural – drained, lifeless, almost as if covered in a layer of the fine, pale dust that settled on everything in that dusty place. You could see their skins would never tan, that the sun would bleach them further, not colour them. It was impossible to imagine that they could share passions and thoughts and feelings with the other people in that hotel garden.

The five of them, mother, father, three girls, walked past the wedding party, under the tight white buds of orange blossom, past the showy poinsettias to a further lawn beyond. Two of the girls linked arms, needing to feel a sister's nearness among so much that was alien. The third child seemed to walk in a dream. She had been the one who had shown no interest in the scramble for sweets. Now her sisters, in obedience to their father's wish, turned somersaults on the grass, performed handstands, showing neat pink knickers. She stood unmoving.

There was an announcement over the hotel loudspeaker: Iraqi Airways Flight Number 247 was leaving for Baghdad. Passengers were requested, in both Arabic and English, to go straight to the Customs Hall.

The first lawn emptied. Black robed women, dark suited men, dozens of colourful children thronged the railings to say goodbye. The bride (still in that white dress) and the groom (their boarding passes sticking out of his top pocket) walked up the steps of the terrace and through to the Customs Hall. The green and white Iraqi Airways buses pulsed in the sunlight.

It was evidently not the American family's plane. The two somersaulting children rushed hand in hand to the railings with the local children. The movement was natural, unconsidered. The dark children did not notice them. They were too busy trying to spot the departing couple as they came out to the airline bus. The pale parents sauntered back along the path, their third daughter trailing behind them. The bright wrapping papers on the lawn were litter now.

'Karen, why don't you?' the mother's voice, weary, worried.

'I'm okay,' Karen said. 'I don't have to.'

She came and sat at the table next to me, tracing her name aimlessly in the dust. I smiled at her, wondering if I might break the unwritten rule and speak. But she gave me no encouragement.

The noise from the wedding party rose again as the young couple came down the path beyond the railings. They walked among the other passengers as if set apart by their new clothes and the day's ceremony. The drumbeats quickened. There were shouts and cries.

The child at the table did not look up. She undid the straps of her denim bag and took out her colouring book. I sipped my orange juice; the ice clinked against the side of the glass. Karen took out a felt pen, licked the end (I could see the dark brown on her tongue) and filled in the faces of the people in her picture.

***

I saw the family again that evening in the foyer of the hotel – they came and sat in the group of chairs next to mine. We had all, I suppose, moved in from the garden to avoid the mosquitoes and the shrill clamour of the small birds which roosted in the tamarisk trees each evening. The branches were thick with birds like September apple trees in a good year just before the picking.

The bare floorboards of the foyer were grey with dust. The upholstery of the chairs was covered in thick plastic to protect it from that dust. Above us, like the propellers of ancient Dakotas, hung six huge fans – not moving, perhaps because it was still only March, perhaps because they did not work. People were coming and going all the time: Kurds in long coats, Turkish footballers in tracksuits, Japanese in the grey uniform of some construction company, Marsh Arabs with their chequered head coverings, Gulf Arabs splendid in flowing robes. There was nothing very remarkable about it. You can see such people any day of the week in Oxford Street, buying courtelle shirts and acrilan trousers to take home and drip dry under a blazing sun. There was nothing very strange about them. But we watched, four of the American family and I, from our uncomfortable shiny chairs. After all, that is what travel is about – looking, observing, noticing, from the outside.

The third child, Karen still did not accept this. She showed no curiosity at all. She fiddled with the thick plastic on her chair. It was already torn. She tore it a little more. A piece came off in her hand and she stared at it as if she would like to make something with it – but what could you make with a transparent piece of plastic, two inches by five? With her other hand, she scratched at a mosquito bite.

In the group of chairs on the other side of the American family there was a plump elderly Arab with a transistor radio at his ear – one of those little ones, no bigger than a packet of cigarettes, bright red and pretty. He was entranced. Something on the radio was giving him pleasure. He sat there, his long robe just touching the dusty floorboards, completely absorbed in what he was hearing. But then there was a slight bang. We all looked across to see what had happened – even Karen. Perhaps he had fallen asleep for a moment, as old people do, and the radio had slipped from his fingers. Anyway, there it was, split open, silent, lying on the floor.

He bent down with difficulty (he was very plump) to pick it up. He looked at it, puzzled and sad. He put the back on again and twiddled with the knob, It was still silent.

Then, to my surprise, Karen had slipped out of her chair (the small piece of plastic falling from her fingers) and went across to him. 'Let me,' she said, 'I know about radios.' And it was apparent that she did. She opened the back again, took a small tool out of the pocket of her denim bag, turned a screw, connected a wire, put the back on again and twiddled with the knobs. And there was music.

She had turned it on rather loud and it seemed that the dusty room was full of it and everyone was smiling and talking and laughing. And for a moment, we were all not observers, not outsiders, but part of things.

And then the announcement came in Arabic and English. Iraqi Airways Flight No. 248 was leaving for Kuwait. Would passengers please… The five of them picked up their bags and started to leave the airport hotel.

The Dog in the Water Meadow

THE MILL STOOD HIGH IN A LOW LANDSCAPE. White, weather-boarded, a landmark for miles around, it rose above low-lying water meadows, where cows grazed and alders and sallows bordered the wandering river. There had been a mill near the site for at least nine centuries; it was recorded in the Domesday Book. For nine hundred years the water had turned the wheel and the millstone had ground the corn and people had paid the miller and baked and eaten the bread.

Now in the 1980s, there was no longer a need for watermills – the corn was contained in huge silos, three or four miles away, and ground by mechanical means. Everything was done with efficiency, on a much larger scale. The Mill was put on the market, developed by a developer, converted into a desirable residence and advertised at a large price by the agent for country properties in the nearest market town. The agent had put his advertisements in the national Sunday papers and people had come from London – in Volvos and Peugeots and Cortinas full of children and dogs – to be shown over the interesting place, trying to imagine their own lives in these totally different surroundings. There was water all round and under the house, if you could call it a house. The river, controlled by a sluice gate, poured under the foundations, under the room which was to be someone's living room – and into the mill pond. The noise was varied according to how much rain there had been, for the river was only a few miles from its source and was considerably affected by the rainfall. But there was always some noise, and people looking over the mill, with the agent pointing out its unique features, found this noise strange, used as they were to the different continuous noise of London traffic.

They worried, of course, that the place would be damp, would give them rheumatism, that their children (some not even at the armband stage) would fall in the river or the mill pond, and drown. They worried too about the Mill's remoteness. The village, which had once clustered round the Mill and the church, had moved at the time of the Black Death. It was now well over a mile away. And the church was closed, redundant, the windows boarded up against vandals, the graves (except those of the recent dead, whose relatives came to tend them) lost among nettles. There would be no five-minutes stroll to the pub in the evening; no shops close at hand if you ran out of butter. The only neighbours were in the Mill House, where the millers had lived and where now (happening to have heard of it before it came on the open market and liking its low comfortable solidity more than the towering Mill) the local manager of a national building society had made his home.

The Mill was on the market for over six months. The people at the Mill House – the manager, his wife, his three adolescent children – had got used to the Mill's emptiness, had given up asking the agent if anyone was interested. Then one spring Saturday when Simon Craft, aged fourteen, was idly banging a tennis ball against the back wall of the stables (now garages) where once the miller's horses had sheltered, a gleaming white car drew up with a spray of gravel, outside the door of the Mill. A man, two smallish children and a large black dog jumped out of the car. A woman followed more slowly. The dog leapt, barked, pleased to be out of the confined space. The children rushed to the bridge above the sluice gate, rushed back to pick up handfuls of gravel, and then threw them in the river with shouts of pleasure at the splashes. A girl of six, perhaps, and a boy of eight, acting as a team.

The man shouted in all directions. 'Sit!' he shouted at the dog, who sat for a second and then bounded off again. 'Get away from the water!' he shouted at the children. 'Stop throwing gravel!'

The woman stood gazing up at the Mill, with her hands over her ears, as if used to the noise and to cutting herself off from it.

Simon had not hit his ball since the car arrived but had stood at the edge of the scene. The rest of his family had gone into the market town for a Saturday morning expedition after shoes. Simon felt there was some need for a reaction though the newcomers hadn't noticed him.

He went across politely to the woman, the quietest, the most approachable. 'Can I help at all?' he said. She didn't hear him at first, with her hands over her ears and all her attention focused on the white Mill, towering above them. Then she saw him and turned and said quietly, as if to herself, 'It could be a new start.'

Before Simon had time to think of an appropriate reply, another car arrived and the estate agent joined them. 'Mrs Fuller?' he asked. 'I'm so sorry to have kept you waiting. I was held up.' He pulled a key out of his pocket and opened the door of the Mill. As they disappeared into the house, the man still seemed to be shouting at the children, though he might have thought he was talking. The dog, now on a lead, was still barking.

Simon, standing outside with his tennis racquet and ball, muttered under his breath, 'I hope they don't take it.'

* * *

But they did. After six months with the Fuller family as neighbours, Simon's forebodings had been well justified. There was always noise. Above the pleasant sound of water, there were less pleasant sounds. The dog, a Doberman Pinscher called Heinrich, smooth haired and menacing, continued to bark. He was often left alone, chained up in a small courtyard at the side of the Mill. Then he would bark, intermittently, until the family returned. It was a sad, useless sound, unrelated to any comings and goings from the Mill House.

As a guard dog, he was useless, for his barking gave warning of nothing but his own frustration.

But worse than Heinrich's bark were the sounds of family anger. Even the silence seemed menacing, likely as it was to be broken at any moment by slamming voices, by arguments and protests. The children, Amy and Peter, who had seemed to Simon on that first day lively and adventurous, became subdued and sullen. Everything they did seemed to irritate one of their parents.

Passing the Mill on their way to the school bus, Simon and his sisters would hear a raised voice from within the Mill in the traditional threat, 'Wait until I tell your father!' The Fuller family had two cars and the children left the house later than the Crafts (driven by their mother to a private school in town) and returned earlier.

Coming home, the Crafts would hurry past the Mill, reluctant to overhear whatever was going on. 'All families quarrel,' Mrs Craft had said soon after the Fullers' arrival. 'Don't take any notice,' she had told them. 'It's not our business.'

It was particularly difficult for Simon not to notice. His room, where he spent so much of his time when he was not at school, was at the Mill end. From his window, he could see, beyond the bridge, the door of the Mill. He could also look into the courtyard where Heinrich barked, circling round and round on his chain whenever the family had left him alone. The boy would turn up the sound on his record player until one of his sisters would come in from their room next door and shout at *him*, 'For heaven's sake, Simon, can't you keep Dire Straits to yourself.' For his birthday, he begged for a Sony Walkman and got one. With that in his ears, he could cut out the outside world, but his schoolwork suffered. It was difficult to write a good essay on the agriculture of the Southern United States with David Bowie going at full blast in his ears.

One night he was woken by a car scrunching over the gravel. He looked automatically at the luminous dial on his alarm clock. It showed twenty minutes past one. A few minutes later there was a sound he could not identify – a queer splattering sound. Someone, he suddenly realised, was throwing gravel at a window. Not his window, but near enough for him to hear it quite distinctly. He opened the window quietly and leaned out. He could see Mrs Fuller standing in front of the Mill. As he watched, she stopped and picked up another handful of gravel and threw it at one of the top floor windows. She had apparently forgotten her key and was trying to rouse her husband.

Minutes passed and nothing happened. She threw another handful. Simon was just beginning to wonder whether there was something he should do – such as offering her the chance of sleeping in the Mill House spare bed – when a window in the Mill opened and Mr Fuller leant out.

'What the bloody hell do you think you're playing at?' Simon could hear the hissed words quite clearly. And Mrs Fuller's simple response, 'Please, Dick... '

Eventually, at long last, after more angry words which he could not quite catch, the Mill door opened and the woman went in. Simon shut his window. The hands on his clock showed that it was nearly quarter to two.

* * *

There were other incidents. Once, on a warm September evening, Simon found Amy and Peter hiding behind a bush at the bottom of the Mill House garden. 'What are you playing at?' he asked them cheerfully. But he could see it was not a game. At first, the children said nothing, then Peter muttered 'We've run away.'

Amy said, 'We have blackberries for our supper.' Her mouth was already stained with blackberry juice. 'Dougal came too,' she added, showing Simon a toy dog. 'He doesn't bark.'

'Heinrich wouldn't bark if he wasn't always being chained up,' Peter said. 'He hates it. I would too.'

'He doesn't like blackberries,' Amy said.

'And what will you have for breakfast?' Simon asked.

'Hazelnuts,' Peter said, after a moment's thought.

Simon picked up a handful from deep in the long grass under the hazel trees, along the river bank. 'How will you open them?' The children looked at the green nuts in their shells in the palm of Simon's hand. He said, 'I'd rather have eggs and bacon.'

'We don't have eggs and bacon. Mummy doesn't have time.'

'Cornflakes, then.'

'Yes, cornflakes,' Peter said.

'And Rice Krispies with milk and sugar on them,' Amy added.

'I think you'd better go home.'

They went quite willingly with him up the Mill House garden, across the bridge. Outside the Mill, they paused, reluctant to go any further. Simon could hear their parents' voices, high, angry, unceasing.

'They haven't even noticed you've gone. Go in the back and slip upstairs to bed. It will be okay in the morning.' He saw Amy's face, stained with blackberries and perhaps tears as well. 'You've had your supper, haven't you? Don't forget to wash your face and clean your teeth.'

The simple instructions, in Simon's kind voice, seemed to calm them. They disappeared round the corner of the Mill.

* * *

Sometimes in the holidays Peter Fuller would be allowed to take Heinrich for a walk along the river, across the water meadows. The boy was growing and getting stronger and learning how to control the dog, which seemed to sense his affection. He had heard Barbara Woodhouse encouraged people to gaze into their animal's eyes. His mother had several times found Peter gazing into Heinrich's eyes when he was supposed to be doing something else.

'You haven't emptied the rubbish,' she would say, impatiently. And the boy would leave the dog and go and do what he was told.

Taking Heinrich for a walk was one way of getting out of the house and actually pleasing his mother at the same time. But he was not supposed to let the dog off the lead. 'He'll kill a chicken or something,' Mrs Fuller said. 'And then the farmer will have your guts for garters.' Peter wasn't sure what she meant but it sounded horrible anyway.

For days that Easter holidays, a year after they had bought the Mill, Peter obeyed his mother. Then one morning, he decided to test his control over the dog. In the house, when Peter told Heinrich to sit, he sat until Peter said 'OK'. On walks, with the choke chain, he had trained Heinrich not to try to bolt after anything that rushed in the undergrowth. The dog still barked endlessly when chained in the courtyard, but with Peter he was becoming well trained and sensible.

There were certainly no chickens about when Peter released Heinrich from his lead. At first, there was no cause for alarm. The dog rushed off but returned immediately when he heard Peter's voice. Peter told him to sit and fastened the lead. They walked on a little further. And again Peter released the dog and again the dog responded obediently to his voice.

They were on their way back to the Mill, when Peter decided to give Heinrich one last taste of freedom. But when he called this time, there was no sign of the dog. Peter rushed in the direction of the Mill, the way the animal had gone. Perhaps he had just gone home. But when Peter came to a gate in a hedge he saw cows in a field by the millpond for the first time that year. And in among the cows, Heinrich – rushing around, ecstatic, barking with pleasure at the great black and white beasts.

'Heinrich!' Peter felt his own voice could hardly be heard for the noise the dog itself was making. 'Heinrich!' he shouted again and kept on shouting. But it was no good. The dog took no notice of him at all.

There was nothing the boy could do but run back to the Mill to tell his mother.

Mrs. Fuller heard what Peter told her and said nothing except, 'Stay with Amy.' She went to a cupboard and unlocked it. She took out a 12-bore shotgun with which her husband occasionally shot rabbits. She put the gun carefully together and loaded it. She did what she had seen him do. Then she went out to the field and called the dog herself. 'Heinrich!' She called three times and he did not respond. The cows were agitated by now. They were themselves bellowing as if in pain, though the dog had not touched them.

The woman raised the gun and fired and the dog fell to the ground. She had always been a good shot. For years she had won hideous china vases at funfairs. The dog was dead; there was no doubt about that.

Simon, alone in the Mill House, heard the shot and rushed outside to see what was going on. So he heard the woman's anguished wail that followed the shot, as if she was weeping for all the destruction and pain in the world, for all the hopes unrealised and promises unfulfilled.

At the window of the Mill, which overlooked the scene, Simon saw the faces of the two children. He ran inside and was with them as, after their first shock, they started to weep themselves.

* * *

Two weeks later, opening the Sunday paper and casually scanning the advertisements for Country Properties, Mr. Craft, local manager of a national building society, turned to his wife. 'The Mill's on the market again,' he said.

The Picnic

IT'S NATURAL THAT PEOPLE LIKE TO spend time alone with their friends sometimes. I do myself. My best friend is called Felicity and we often like to do things by ourselves, without our brothers barging in and without our mums telling us what we should do and shouldn't do. But that day, Felicity's mum was a problem in a different way. *She* wanted to spend time with her friend Ralph and she didn't want Felicity or Paul (that's Felicity's little brother), she didn't want them barging in and making nuisances of themselves. Above all, she didn't want them to annoy Ralph.

I'm not sure why (there are quite a lot of things I'm not sure about) but Ralph has got the idea that he doesn't like children. This seems silly to me. I mean it's like saying you don't like people. There are some nice children and some silly children, some interesting ones and some boring ones, and you shouldn't lump the whole lot together.

Anyway, that day, the day I'm telling you about, Felicity's mum had got it into her head that Felicity and Paul might keep out of Ralph's way if they had

Adam (that's my brother) and me over to play. She rang up our mum and said she'd give us a picnic lunch and we could take it anywhere in the grounds and have a lovely time. She didn't say anything about us keeping out of their way. But I knew that that was what it was really all about.

Not that I minded being invited to have a picnic with Felicity and Paul. In fact, I liked the idea a lot. The thing that makes Ralph special – and is one reason I think why Felicity's mum is so keen on him – is that he lives all alone in the most enormous house you ever saw. I suppose you would call it a 'stately home'. It has hundreds of rooms – well, dozens anyway. There's a huge hall with fireplaces at both ends and there's a library and funny rooms that no one else has, like a gun-room and a butler's pantry and a servants' hall – though there aren't any servants now, only a couple of dailies who come in from the village.

In the village we always call Ralph's house Sheepworth, but Felicity's mum calls it 'The Hall', because I suppose it sounds grander when she mentions it casually to other people who don't know Sheepworth and might think it was just the name of a village, not a house, if she called it just that, like everyone else.

So there was Felicity's mum ringing up our mum and asking us round to 'The Hall' for a picnic. Moreover, she said, if we could find a really good place in the grounds and all went well, maybe Paul and I could have a special birthday picnic there with some of our friends when our birthdays came, within a day of each other, at the end of the month.

Adam and I walked round to Sheepworth at half past eleven. Felicity and Paul were looking out for us at the end of the drive – the drive is so long you can't even see the house from the end. They were swinging on the great iron gates and I remember thinking that was just the sort of thing that would make Ralph think he didn't like children.

I knew him quite well, you see. Long before Felicity and Paul and their mum came to live in our village, Ralph used to come round to our cottage sometimes and see our mum and dad. They used to go to Sheepworth, too; they still do.

They've always been friends and that's why it makes me a bit mad when Felicity talks as if Sheepworth is her special place. Not that she really likes it all that much. Sometimes she and Paul sleep there in the nursery wing, miles away from the rest of the house, and she says it's really spooky.

They have bats at Sheepworth and Nick Tyler at school says it's haunted by the ghost of a man called Frederick Tupper. He was the butler in Ralph's mother's time and he drowned himself in the lake. Dad says that it's nonsense about ghosts, but it's true, he had to admit it, that the butler was drowned. That wasn't long before I was born.

It was even a bit spooky that day as we walked down the drive at Sheepworth with Felicity and Paul. It was May but not a bright day. Trees crowded the drive and even if there had been sun we would have been in shadow. Felicity and Paul had a great basket full of food, covered with a checked tea towel. They started telling us what was in it because they watched their mum pack it. It was a really smart picnic – suitable for eating in the grounds of 'The Hall' and not the sort of packed lunch we get to take to school. Not sandwiches, but pieces of cooked chicken and pork pies and whole tomatoes, chocolate biscuits, little pots of orange mousse and fizzy lemonade pretending to be champagne.

When Adam heard what was in the picnic basket, he suggested we sat down and ate it where we were, in among the buttercups and cow parsley, under the trees. But Felicity reminded him we were supposed to be finding a special picnic place, and it was only if we did – and one well away from the house – that we would be allowed to ask our friends from school to the special birthday picnic.

Paul said, 'I'd rather go to *Flash Gordon* and have a Wimpy.'

'It's not still on, silly,' Felicity said. That had been Gary Carpenter's birthday treat two weeks before.

We trailed down the drive and along a path, avoiding the house as we had been told. We took turns to carry the basket and it got heavier and heavier. The sky, which had been grey, was now black and suddenly large drops of rain began to fall. Adam and I had our anoraks on but Felicity and Paul only had tee-shirts and, by the time we got to the house for shelter, they were both quite wet and cold. Paul is only small and he started whimpering a bit and Felicity started shouting 'Mum! Mum!' just as if she were at home.

The house is so big you can never find anyone in it. We tried the library first, but there wasn't anyone there. We walked across the polished floor of the hall, down a long passage and through the kitchens and sculleries, and there wasn't anyone anywhere. Paul went on whimpering and Felicity went on shouting. Adam and I carried the basket between us and kept quiet.

Eventually we went upstairs to the drawing room and Paul forgot for a moment how cold and wet he was by making funny faces in the mirrors. I carefully picked up a few blades of grass that had come off our shoes and on to the beautiful rugs. Persian, I think you call them.

'Mum!' Felicity called again. A few minutes later their mum appeared, looking flustered and rather cross.

'What on earth are you all doing here?' She demanded. 'I told you to have a picnic.'

'It's raining,' Felicity said flatly. 'Hadn't you noticed?'

'I'm cold.' Paul said.

Adam and I kept quiet. I stooped and picked up another blade of grass so that I didn't have to look at Felicity's mum while she tried to think how to get rid of us.

'Can't you see it's raining?' Felicity repeated.

Her mum looked out of the window. 'So it is. What a rotten day for a picnic.' Then she said brightly 'It's the sort of day that needs enterprise and imagination. You can have a special wet-day picnic – a picnic where no-one has ever had a picnic before.'

'Where?' Felicity asked,

'I'm cold,' Paul said.

'Susan!' Ralph called from a room nearby. I don't think I ever knew before that Felicity's mum was called Susan.

Adam and I said nothing. Felicity's mum was looking more cheerful and determined.

'Go down to the kitchen and get your jerseys and anoraks. They're on that chair by the Aga. Remember? Put them on. Then go round to the old laundry and have your picnic there. It's nearly lunchtime now. Have fun.'

We obediently trooped down to the kitchen. It was nice and warm in there because of the Aga. Paul peeled off his tee-shirt and put on his dry clothes. So did Felicity. Adam and I were okay but I thought it would have been quite good to stay in the warm room and have our picnic on the kitchen table. But we didn't dare.

Anyway, we were all quite keen to explore the old laundry. There were lots of outbuildings round a sort of yard at the side of the house: stables (with no horses in them), harness-rooms (with no harnesses), dairies, potting sheds and this old laundry which was no longer needed now there was a washing machine in one of the sculleries. We weren't normally allowed to go round there because some of the buildings were falling down and I suppose Ralph was worried we might get hit on the head by a falling tile and sue him for damages.

But today was different, apparently. Felicity's mum has said we could use the old laundry. In fact she had *told* us we should eat our picnic there. We walked across the yard and tried the door of the old laundry. It was locked.

'Oh, no!' we all said it together.

'What do we do now?' Adam asked 'We can't go and find your mum again.'

'Look,' said Felicity. There's a broken pane in that window.' It was quite near the window latch. 'Can you reach it, Adam?' He was the tallest but even he couldn't. We looked around for something for him to climb on and there was one of those wooden crates that bottles sometimes come in.

Adam stood on it and put his hand through the broken pane and was able to open the window. With the help of the crate, he climbed in and opened the door from inside and let the rest of us in.

It wasn't a very good place for a picnic. For a start, it smelt musty and fusty in spite of the broken pane. Splinters of glass sprinkled the floor. There was a huge old copper that they used to do the washing in. It would have been quite good for the three little pigs to boil the wolf in, but no one wanted to be the wolf. We could sympathise with his hunger.

We sat down on the dusty floor, careful to avoid the glass. We spread the tea towel out in the middle and unpacked the picnic food. Felicity's mum had put in paper plates with Snoopy on them and the food tasted good. There were paper cups with Charlie Brown on them and Felicity poured out fizzy lemonade. Paul knocked his over and it made such interesting patterns in the dusty floor that he couldn't resist trailing his fingers through them. Then somehow his fingers got near his face. He was very dirty.

After the orange mousse and the chocolate biscuits, Felicity tried the tap over the old copper and a few rusty drops came out. She tried to wash Paul with them.

'I'd better clean him up before Ralph sees him,' she said. But somehow he looked almost worse when she had finished.

However, of course, we all felt better when we had eaten and better still when we came out of the old laundry and found that the rain had stopped and there were even some gleams of sun. We packed the basket with the Snoopy plates, the Charlie Brown paper cups, the mousse pots and chicken bones and covered them neatly with the checked towel. Paul's lemonade had dried and the old laundry looked much the same as it had when we arrived.

We put the basket just inside the kitchen door and rushed across the yard and the lawns and into the lovely woods. Suddenly it seemed a good day – a day for remembering it was Saturday and no school again tomorrow.

* * *

It was only when Adam and I were lying comfortably reading and I was feeling I would go to sleep in a minute, when I heard the doorbell and then someone talking in the room below. Our cottage is very old and although the walls are thick, the floors are thin and you can hear everything people are saying in the room below, unless they talk very quietly, as Mum and Dad generally do. Now someone was talking in a rather loud, hectic voice and I could hear every word. It was Felicity's mum.

'I'm sorry,' she was saying, but she didn't sound sorry, more embarrassed and a bit shifty. 'I'm sorry to have to tell you Adam disgraced himself today. Ralph is very angry. I'm afraid Adam broke into the old laundry and let the other children in, and he knows, they all know, that Ralph has said they are *never* to play round there. It's very dangerous. They might have been killed.'

I couldn't believe my ears, but there was no doubt at all that Felicity's mum was putting all the blame on Adam. She never said that it was *she* who had told us to have our picnic there. It was all her idea.

I could hear Mum and Dad muttering in a worried sort of way. Then the front door slammed shut – Felicity's mum had apparently gone – and I could hear Dad's feet on the stairs and then the sound of Dad rushing into Adam's room and thumping him. Adam yelled and leapt out of bed with Dad's other hand still on his arm and I rushed in and we were both shouting to Dad to stop and hear our side of the story.

He let Adam go and sat down on the side of the bed and put his head in his hands. When we'd finished, he said very quietly, 'I'm sorry. I believe you.'

'Felicity's mum is a liar,' I said. 'I hate her.'

'Don't be too hard on her,' Dad said. 'She was afraid to tell Ralph she had given you permission.'

'So she blamed a boy,' I said, putting as much scorn into my voice as I could. 'What a horrible thing to do.'

Dad sighed and murmured 'Some people do horrible things when they are in love. There's a saying – do you know it? All's fair in love and war… '

'In love?' I repeated the words. Felicity's mum in love with Ralph? I didn't want to think about it, they were so old.

There was only one thing I knew for certain. Paul and I wouldn't be sharing a special birthday picnic in the grounds of Sheepworth Hall that May. Nor any May if I had anything to do with it.

Jack's Poem

There is a man who cannot stand fat meat,
Who (with his Jill) went uphill on his feet,
Who joins a Union, then makes a flag,
Who lives inside a box and not a bag,
Who is a jolly sailor (and a rabbit),
Who climbs a beanstalk, and who makes a habit
Of eating plums in puddings. You could play
A sort of dressed-up chimneysweep in May,
Or games with him – when turned into five stones.
Or he becomes an animal that groans
Ee-aw Ee-aw, and then a bird
Much like a thieving crow. His name's a word
That goes with lanterns, offices, pots, boots,
Lifts cars, makes frost, can cut, diverts planes' routes.
He killed a frightful Giant. Though not a master
Of trades at all, his diving is much faster
Than any bellyflop. In politics
He was called Straw, a man of knavish tricks.
Robinson's one name – but, tell me, can you say
Something before it which gives my game away?

Anthony Thwaite

About the Author

ANN THWAITE is the author of five major biographies. *A. A. Milne: His Life* was the Whitbread Biography of the Year, 1990. *Edmund Gosse: A Literary Landscape* (Duff Cooper Prize, 1985) was described by John Carey as 'magnificent – one of the finest literary biographies of our time'. *Glimpses of the Wonderful* about the life of Edmund's father, Philip Henry Gosse, was picked out by D. J. Taylor in the *Independent* as one of the 'Ten Best Biographies' ever. *Beyond the Secret Garden: the life of Frances Hodgson Burnett* was originally published (1974) as *Waiting for the Party* and reissued in 2007. *Emily Tennyson, The Poet's Wife* (1996) was reissued by Faber Finds for the Tennyson bicentenary in 2009.

Two of her biographies, those of A. A. Milne and Frances Hodgson Burnett, are available as e-books.

Born in London, Ann spent the war years in New Zealand, returning to complete her education at Queen Elizabeth's, Barnet, and St Hilda's College, Oxford. She has lived in Tokyo, Benghazi and Nashville, Tennessee. She has lectured in many countries, but most of her life has been spent as a writer. She is an Oxford D.Litt, and a Fellow of the Royal Society of Literature; and has an honorary doctorate from the University of East Anglia.

For forty years, Ann Thwaite wrote children's books, including *The Camelthorn Papers* (1969), translated into Japanese and Greek, *Tracks,* a New Zealand story, and several much-loved picture books, including *Gilbert and the Birthday Cake, The Day with the Duke* and *The Horse at Hilly Fields.* Jan Mark included her story 'Feeding the Cats' in the *Oxford Book of Children's Stories* (1993).

From 1968 to 1975, Ann Thwaite edited the children's annual *Allsorts,* for which she commissioned many of the leading writers and illustrators for children, but also other writers (for instance, Michael Frayn and William Trevor), who had never written for children before. For over thirty years she was on the editorial board of the American Children's Magazine group, which published *Cricket, Ladybug* and *Spider.*

She reviewed children's books, mainly in *The Times Literary Supplement*, for many years, and ran a library for local children in her home.

The Brilliant Career of Winnie-the Pooh, a scrapbook offshoot of her Milne biography, was published on both sides of the Atlantic in 1992. *My Oxford* (1977) contained memories of their time there by writers including John Mortimer, Antonia Fraser, and Martin Amis. Her edition of *Portraits from Life* is a collection (1991) of Edmund Gosse's essays on his friends, including Henry James, Robert Louis Stevenson and Thomas Hardy.

Ann Thwaite's most recent book is a history of her own family: *Passageways, the story of a New Zealand family* (2009), and much praised on both sides of the world. All eight of her great-grandparents emigrated to New Zealand in the middle of the nineteenth century and it was the realisation that she knew so much more about the families of her biographical subjects that made her look into her own family history.

She has lived for most of the last forty years in Norfolk with her husband, the poet Anthony Thwaite.

Lightning Source UK Ltd.
Milton Keynes UK
UKOW04n1424091217
314180UK00001B/132/P